هدية لجيتا

A GIFT FOR GITA

by Rachna Gilmore

Illustrated by Alice Priestley

Arabic Translation by Azza Habashi

mantra

لمست جيتا الوجة الامع الناعم لعروستها الخشبية. لقد أحبت كيف
تُفتح هذه اللعبة من حول المركز لتظهر بداخلها عروسة أخرى
بداخلها عروسة أخرى... وهكذا سبعة بكاملها. احضرتها جدتها
نانيجى من الهند. لقد كانت زيارتها الأولى منذ رحلت جيتا وأمها
وأبوها ثلاث سنوات مضت.

Gita touched the smooth face of the bright, wooden doll.
She loved how it opened around the centre with another
doll inside and another inside that - seven in all. Naniji, her
grandmother, had brought it from India. It was her first
visit since Gita, Mum and Dad had left three years ago.

لقد فعلوا تقريباً كل شئ خططت له جيتا، مشوا بجوار القناة عند الفجر، وعسكروا مع أحسن صديقاتها إيمى، وصنعوا نانيجى آيس كريم المانجو اللذيذ.

حضنت جيتا نانيجى وقالت "يجب أن تجربى التزحلق على الجليد. سوف تحبينه." ابتسمت نانيجى وقالت: "لا لا! أليس يكفي اننى نزلت إلى هذا القارب، مع أنكم حاولتم أن تغرقونى؟"

فانفجرت جيتا وأمها في الضحك؟

They'd done nearly everything Gita'd planned - walked along the canal at dawn, camped with her best friend Amy, made Naniji's delicious mango ice cream.

Gita hugged Naniji. "You have to try ice-skating. You'll love it."

Naniji chuckled. "Oh no! Isn't it enough that I got into that boat, even though you tried to drown me?"

Mum and Gita burst out laughing.

"هل أحضرت الصور التى أخذناها في المخيم يا أبى؟ الصور التى صورتها لنا نانيجى في القرب؟"

كان الأب يقف بجوار النافذة يقرأ خطاباً. رفع رأسه وقال "أنا آسف يا جيتا، لقد نسيت."

نظرت جيتا إلى أبيها عن قرب. ماذا حدث؟

"Dad, did you get the pictures of our camping trip yet? The ones of Naniji in the boat?"

Dad was standing by the window, reading a letter. He looked up. "I'm sorry, Gita, I forgot."

Gita looked at Dad closely. What was the matter?

طوى الأب الخطاب وجلس. ثم نظر إلى نانيجى وسلك حنجرته. وقال "لقد عرضت علىَّ وظيفة أفضل. ولكن، ولكن، قد نضطر إلى أن ننتقل." "ننتقل؟ أين؟" سألت الأم بصوت حاد.

"نعود إلى الهند" أجاب الأب بهدوء.

نعود إلى الهند وإلى نانيجى! انشرح قلب جيتا من الفرح. ثم ببطء عبس قلبها ونزل إلى أطراف قدميها.

أترك إيمى، وهذا البيت، وصديقاتها؟

Dad folded the letter and sat down. He glanced at Naniji, then cleared his throat.

"I've been offered a better job. But, but, we would have to move."

"Move? Where?" Mum's voice was sharp.

"Back to India," said Dad quietly.

Back to India and Naniji! Gita's heart leapt with delight. Then slowly it sank to her toes. Leave Amy, this house, her friends?

لقد كان صمت طويل.

"سوف تقبل هذه الوظيفة؟ أليس كذلك؟ سألت نانيجى.

نظرت جيتا إلى وجه أمها الشاحب، وأعين أبيها الخاشعتين.

"انه شيء يجب علينا جميعاً أن نتخذ قراراً بشأنه. لقد مكثنا هنا ثلاث سنوات الآن، وزرعنا جذوراً." نظرت جيتا إلى نانيجى. كانت تبتسم ولكن إبتسامة كتلك التى كانت تبتسمها عندما كنا نرحل عن الهند. جرت جيتا خارج المنزل إلى مخبأها تحت شجرتها المفضلة.

There was a long silence.
"You will take the job, won't you?" asked Naniji.
Gita stared at Mum's pale face, Dad's downcast eyes.
Dad said slowly, "It's something we all have to decide. We've been here for three years now. We've put down roots."
Gita looked at Naniji. She was smiling - but the way she had smiled when they were leaving India. Gita ran outside to her hiding place under her favourite tree.

عندما انتقلت أولاً هنا، كيف حزنت على ترك منزلها في الهند.
أعندما بدأت أن تفقد حنينها إليه؟ وعندما توطدت صداقتها بإيمى؟
وعندما ذهبت لأول مرة على الجليد؟ فتحت جيتا عروستها،
أخرجت أجزاءها حتى القلب، لقد كانت مثل ما كان يُحدث
بداخلها، ذكريات كثيرة جداً – اللعب بالدوارة، المخيم، زراعة
الورد مع السيد فلنش جارهم... الهند الآن بالنسبة لها كلون بعيد غير
واضح، أمَّا هنا فكل شئ واضح وكامل، صاخب وآنى.

When she'd first moved here, how she'd ached for her
home in India. Just when had she stopped missing it? When
she and Amy became friends? When she first went
ice-skating? Gita opened her doll, took out each one, right
down to the centre. It was like that inside her, so many
different moments - playing rounders, camping, planting
roses with Mr Flinch next door ... India was now a blur of
distant colour. Here was full and clear, loud and now.

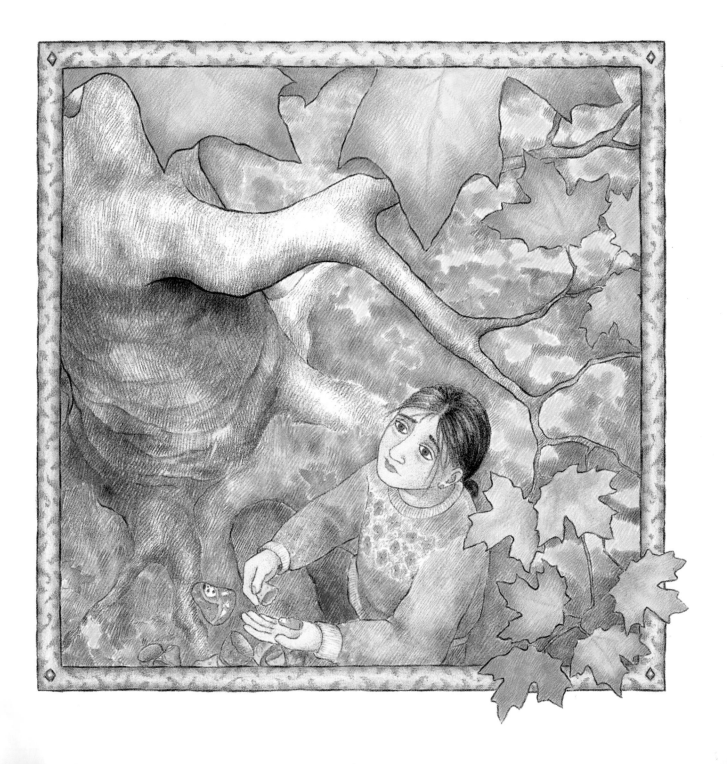

أعادت جيتا اللعب في بعضها. ما أجملها في موضعها المتوافق تماماً
مثل ما تتوافق كل أجزاء كيانها، هنا، حتى ولو من غير نانيجى،
بيتى هنا. ولكن ماذا لو قرر أبى وأمى أن يعودا؟
وجرت إلى الداخل. أصوات الأم والأب ونانيجى خفتت وأصبحت
كأصوات أوراق الشجر وهى تتساقط.

Gita put the dolls back together. How beautifully they
fit. Just like all the parts of her fit - fit here. Even without
Naniji, home was here.
But what if Mum and Dad decided to go back?
She ran inside. The voices of Mum, Dad and Naniji
rustled and swirled like falling leaves.

"أمى، أبى، أنا لا أستطيع أن أذهب، سوف لا أذهب. هذا وطنى، علَّى أن أبقى هنا." طوقتها الأم بذراعيها.

وقال الأب "كل شئ على ما يرام يا جيتا، سوف لا نذهب."

تنفست جيتا الصعداء. "سوف نبقى." ثم نظرت إلى وجه نانيجى.

"Mum, Dad, I can't go, I won't. This is home, I have to stay."

Mum held her close.

"It's all right, Gita," said Dad. "We're not going."

Gita took a deep breath. "We're staying." Then she saw Naniji's face.

"نانيجي أنا أريد أن أكون معك ولكن ..." ضمت جيتا اللعبة إلى
صدرها وقالت:"كل شئ هنا إلاَّ أنت."

ابتسمت الأم وقالت:"جزء مني مازال يفتقد الهند، عائلاتنا، الألوان
الزاهية، عطر الياسمين. ولكننا اخترنا أن نحضر إلى هنا، وكذلك
أحببنا هنا."

"إبقى معنا يا نانيجي، من فضلك." همست جيتا.

"Naniji, I want to be with you, but ..." She held the doll
against her heart. "Everything's here, but you."

Mum smiled. "Part of me still misses India, our families,
oh the colours, the scent of jasmine. But we chose to come
here, and I love it too."

"Stay with us, Naniji," whispered Gita. "Please?"

"وطني هناك في الهند،" قالت نانيجي بهدوء. "أنا أحب أن أعيش هناك، تماماً كما تحبين أنت هنا. إنه هناك حيث عشت كل ذكرياتي، كل أجزائي ... كل شئ إلا أنتم."

"تستطيعين أن، تعيشي ذكريات جديدة هنا."

"عندي مسبقاً." ردت نانيجي "سوف آخذها وأضمها إلى الذكريات التي عشتها معكم هناك. وتذكروا أن جزءً مني معكم دائماً."

"My home is back in India," said Naniji softly. "I love it there, just as you love it here. It's where all my memories are, all the parts of me - everything except you."

"You can make new memories. Here."

"I already have," said Naniji. "To take back and keep with the ones I have of you there. But remember part of me is always with you."

استطاعت جيتا أن تبتسم. نعم، نانيجي كانت هنا تساعد في تقليم الورود، تضحك بينما تمرجح مضرب الدوارة، قائلة أنها تفضل الكريكيت، تلف حولها وحول إيمي ساري لامع. ونانيجي تقص حواديت تحت ضوء النجوم. وجزء من جيتا سوف يكون دائما معها. فتحت جيتا العروسة وأخرجت العرائس كلها من داخلها، وعينيها تطرفان أخرجت أصغر عروسة ووضعتها في يد نانيجي.

Gita managed a smile. Yes, Naniji was here - helping trim roses, laughing, swinging a rounders bat, saying she preferrd cricket, winding brilliant saris around her and Amy. Naniji. Naniji spinning stories under the stars. And part of Gita would always be with her. Gita opened the doll, right to the centre. Eyes stinging, she pressed the smallest doll into Naniji's hand.

عصفت ريح في الخارج جعلت فروع الأشجار ترقص "أنظري،" صاحت جيتا، "أشجاري تحتفل بزيارتك." لمست نانيجي خد جيتا. "وكذلك بيتك."

ابتسمت جيتا ببطئ وهمست، "نعم بيتي."

A gust of wind outside set the branches of her tree dancing.
"Look," said Gita, "my tree's celebrating your visit."
Naniji touched Gita's cheek. "And your home."
Slowly Gita smiled. "Yes, my home," she whispered.

After reading this story, you may wish to think about the following questions:

1. Gita's grandmother lives far away. Where do your grandparents live?

2. How does Gita feel about moving? How would you feel if you had to move to another place?

3. What do you think Gita's gift is?